c.1

E R
HOB

Hoban, Lillian

Arthur's back to
school day

DUE DATE

An I Can Read Book®

Arthur's
Back to School Day

story and pictures by

Lillian Hoban

HarperCollins*Publishers*

HarperCollins®, ®, and I Can Read Book®
are trademarks of HarperCollins Publishers Inc.

Arthur's Back to School Day
Copyright © 1996 by Lillian Hoban
Printed in the U.S.A. All rights reserved.

Library of Congress Cataloging-in-Publication Data
Hoban, Lillian.
   Arthur's back to school day / Lillian Hoban.
      p.   cm. — (An I can read book)
   Summary: While hurrying to get on the school bus, Arthur and his friend
unknowingly switch their lunch boxes; later Arthur finds out what surprise his
sister had put into hers.
   ISBN 0-06-024955-2. — ISBN 0-06-024956-0 (lib. bdg.)
   [1. School buses—Fiction.   2. Lunch boxes—Fiction.   3. Brothers and
sisters—Fiction   4. Chimpanzees—Fiction]   I. Title.   II. Series.
PZ7.H635Are   1996   95-8883
[E]—dc20   CIP
                                                                       AC

                    1   2   3   4   5   6   7   8   9   10
                                    ❖
                              First Edition

For Daniel and Elias

Happy School Days!

It was the first day of school.

Arthur and Violet were waiting

for the school bus.

They had new lunch boxes.

Arthur's was purple and red.

Violet's was pink and yellow.

"I love my lunch box,"

said Violet.

"I love the little plastic box

for snacks."

"Me too," said Arthur.

"I put some baseball cards in mine
so I can trade."

"I put a secret surprise in mine,"
said Violet.

"If you put it in yourself,

you can't be surprised,"

said Arthur.

"Yes I can," said Violet.

"I closed my eyes when I put it in."

7

Norman and his dog, Bubbles,

came down the road.

Bubbles was carrying

Norman's lunch box.

"Look, Arthur," said Violet.

"Norman's lunch box

is just like yours."

"Hey, Arthur," called Norman.

"Do you want to trade

baseball cards?

I got doubles on some good ones."

"Let's see," said Arthur.

Norman took his baseball cards

out of his lunch box.

Arthur took out

his baseball cards too.

10

"Here comes the school bus,"

said Violet.

Arthur quickly put his baseball cards

back in his snack box.

Arthur and Violet got on the bus.

Norman came running

and got on too.

Bubbles ran after him.

"No dogs allowed on the bus,"

said the driver.

He shut the door and drove on.

"Wait!" yelled Norman.

"Bubbles has my lunch box!"

"I can't stop here,"

said the driver.

"Look," said Violet.

"Bubbles is running after the bus."

All the children

stood up to look.

"Come on, Bubbles,"

shouted Arthur. "You can do it!"

"Yay, Bubbles!" everyone cheered.

"Remember your safety rules!"

called the driver.

"No standing or shouting

on the school bus!"

"Oh no," cried Norman.

"Everything is falling

out of my lunch box!"

All the children crowded

to the back of the bus to see.

"Safety rules!" yelled the driver.

"Please go back to your seats."

"There goes your apple, Norman,"

called Arthur.

"It's bouncing down the road."

"I didn't have an apple,"

said Norman.

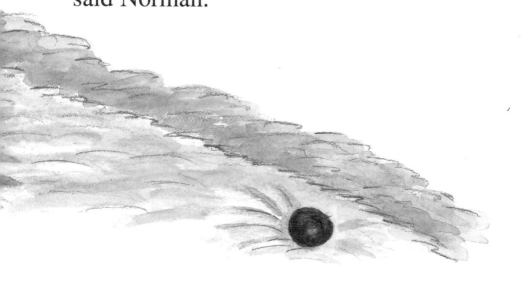

"Norman's snack box

just fell in the dirt,"

said Violet.

"Let me see," said Wilma.

She stood up on the seat.

18

"I can't see Bubbles anymore,"

said Wilma.

"Safety rules! Safety rules!"

yelled the driver.

"No standing on the seats!"

The bus pulled up

in front of the school.

Just then Wilma's big sister, Mabel,

rode up on her bike.

"Whose lunch box is this?"

she asked.

"It's mine! It's mine!"

yelled Norman.

"Your lunch was all over

the road," said Mabel,

"but I put it back

in your lunch box."

20

"I'm glad you got your lunch back,"
said the bus driver,
"but you kids need to learn
your safety rules."
The children got off the bus.

Inside the school

there was a big sign.

It said:

WELCOME to the
NEW
SCHOOL YEAR!

"GOOD MORNING, BOYS AND GIRLS,"

said a voice over the loudspeaker.

"THIS IS YOUR PRINCIPAL, MR. ADAMS.

ALL CLASSES PLEASE COME

TO THE AUDITORIUM."

When they got to the auditorium,

Mr. Adams said,

"Today is the first day of school.

It is important

that you learn some safety rules.

Can anyone give me a safety rule

for riding on the school bus

and tell me why it is important?"

Arthur raised his hand.

"No standing on the bus,"

he said,

"because if the bus hits a bump,

you might fall and get hurt."

Norman raised his hand.

"No pushing or shoving,"

he said,

"because you could get knocked down

and your loose tooth

might get bonked out."

Violet raised her hand.

"No dogs on the bus," she said,

"because the driver

might be scared of dogs

and run off the road."

"Very good," said Mr. Adams.

"Now go back to your classrooms

and write down

all those safety rules

and any more

you can think of."

All the children went

to their new classrooms.

Arthur and Norman went

to Ms. Wilson's class.

On the way

Norman said to Arthur,

"I can't wait for recess

to trade baseball cards."

"I can't wait to eat my snack,"

said Arthur.

"I have an apple and

two chocolate chip cookies."

In the classroom

the children drew pictures

of a school bus.

Arthur colored his bus black.

Under the picture

he wrote all the safety rules

he could think of.

Then he yawned and looked around.

Everyone was still writing.

Arthur closed his eyes.

He thought about his snack.

He could almost taste

the chocolate chips.

Brrr . . . ing! A bell rang.

"Recess," said Ms. Wilson.

"Come on, Arthur,"

said Norman.

"Let's go trade."

Arthur and Norman

took their lunch boxes

out to the school yard.

"Arthur," called Violet,

"I just opened my snack box

and found my secret surprise!"

"Well," said Arthur,

"I know what is in my snack box,

and it is no surprise!"

Arthur opened his lunch box

and took out the snack box.

But he _was_ surprised.

Instead of chocolate chip cookies

there were cheese crackers

under the baseball cards!

"Phooey!" said Arthur.

"This is not my snack."

Norman was looking

in his lunch box.

He held up a dusty apple.

"I can't eat apples,"

he said.

"I have a loose front tooth."

"That's my apple!" said Arthur,

"and that's my lunch!"

Arthur took the lunch box

from Norman.

He looked inside the snack box.

"My chocolate chip cookies

are gone," he cried.

"Bubbles loves

chocolate chip cookies,"

said Norman.

"He probably ate them."

"Oh no!" cried Arthur.

Violet came running over.

She was holding something

behind her back.

"Guess what

my secret surprise is,"

she said.

"Oh phooey!" said Arthur.

"I don't want to guess.

I just want

a chocolate chip cookie!"

"You guessed! You guessed!"

cried Violet.

She held up two

chocolate chip cookies.

"You can have one

because you guessed!"

Arthur ate the cookie

Violet gave him.

He traded baseball cards

with Norman.

Then he went back to class

and had a great first day

in school.

And on the way home

everyone followed

the safety rules

for riding on the school bus.